If you had to choose, would you be a vampire or a fairy?

I would be a fairy because you could flutter around.
— Frankie

I would be a vampire because they are spooky.
— Oliver

Vampire! Because then you can stay up all night and not be told to go to bed.
— Sam

I'd like to be a vampire like Isadora's dad because they eat red food like tomatoes and strawberries.
— Harriet

I like fairies because they are magic!
— Antonia

Fairies are better because they eat lots of cupcakes.
— Ruby

Sink your fangs into an Isadora Moon adventure!

Isadora Moon Goes to School

Isadora Moon Goes Camping

Coming soon!

Isadora Moon Goes to the Ballet

Isadora Moon Has a Birthday

ISADORA MOON

Goes to School

Harriet Muncaster

A STEPPING STONE BOOK™

Random House 🏫 New York

For vampires, fairies, and humans everywhere!
And for Sarah, my glamorous mother-in-law.

Copyright © 2016 by Harriet Muncaster
Cover art copyright © 2016 by Harriet Muncaster

All rights reserved. Published in the United States by Random House Children's Books, a division of Penguin Random House LLC, New York. Originally published in paperback by Oxford University Press, Oxford, in 2016.

Random House and the colophon are registered trademarks and A Stepping Stone Book and the colophon are trademarks of Penguin Random House LLC.

Visit us on the Web!
SteppingStonesBooks.com
randomhousekids.com

Educators and librarians, for a variety of teaching tools, visit us at RHTeachersLibrarians.com

Library of Congress Cataloging-in-Publication Data is available upon request.
ISBN 978-0-399-55821-4 (hc) — ISBN 978-0-399-55822-1 (lib. bdg.)
ISBN 978-0-399-55823-8 (pbk.) — ISBN 978-0-399-55824-5 (ebook)

MANUFACTURED IN CHINA
10 9 8 7 6 5 4 3 2 1
First American Edition

This book has been officially leveled by using the F&P Text Level Gradient™ Leveling System.

ISADORA MOON

Goes to School

Chapter One

Isadora Moon. That's me!

Pink Rabbit and I have lots of fun together.

My mom is Countess Cordelia Moon. She's a fairy. Yes, really! She likes gardening, swimming in wild streams, having magical campfires, and sleeping outdoors under the stars.

My dad is Count Bartholomew Moon. He's a vampire. Yes, really! He likes staying up all night, eating only red food (tomatoes—yuck!), gazing at the night sky with his special telescope, and flying in front of a full moon.

Then there's my little sister, Baby Honeyblossom. She's half-fairy, half-vampire, just like me! She likes sleeping, gurgling, and drinking pink milk.

Pink Rabbit and I do everything together.

He was my favorite stuffed animal, so Mom
cast a spell to make him alive.

And this is our house! That's my bedroom at the top of the tallest tower. I can see the whole town from my window. Pink Rabbit is mostly not allowed to look out the window because he likes jumping off things too much.

He thinks he can fly like me.

He can't fly.

Chapter Two

Every morning I watch the human children walking down the road to school. They wear funny-looking uniforms with striped ties.

And even though the children look very friendly . . .

And even though they look like they are having fun . . .

It makes me glad that I am a vampire-fairy, because vampire-fairies don't have to go to school.

Or so I thought . . .

Yesterday evening I was practicing flying my loop-the-loops out my bedroom window, when Dad called me from downstairs.

"Isadora!" he said. "Breakfast time!"

Dad always has his breakfast at seven o'clock at night because he sleeps during the day. Mom has hers in the morning. This means I usually have two breakfasts. I don't mind, because peanut butter on toast is my favorite thing to eat.

Dad was sitting at the table drinking a glass of his very special red smoothie juice. I think it's disgusting. I do not like red food, especially tomatoes. I know there are tomatoes in Dad's special red smoothie juice.

"One day you'll enjoy it like a real vampire," he says to me. "All vampires love red food."

But I know I won't. I'm only half-vampire, after all.

Mom was there too, opening the kitchen windows to let in the fresh air and putting bunches of flowers in vases.

We have fourteen vases of flowers in the kitchen. And a tree growing from the middle of the floor! Mom just loves to bring the outdoors inside.

Honeyblossom was fussing in her high chair because she had dropped her bottle on the floor. I picked it up for her and filled it with some more pink milk. She hates red juice, just like me.

Dad said, "Isadora, the time has come for you to start school."

"But, Dad," I said, "I am a vampire-fairy. I do not need to go to school."

"Even fairies have to go to school," said Mom.

"Vampires too!" added Dad.

"But I don't *want* to go to school," I said. "I have a perfectly busy and fun life at home with Pink Rabbit."

"But you might enjoy it," insisted Dad. "I used to love my vampire school as a young boy."

"And I adored my fairy school!" said Mom, spooning some flower-nectar yogurt into her bowl.

"You'll have a wonderful time!" They both smiled.

I wasn't so sure.

"But I'm not a full fairy," I said. "And I'm

not a full vampire. So which school would I go to? Is there one especially for vampire-fairies? Is there a school for me?"

"Well . . . no," said Mom. "Not exactly."

"You are very rare," said Dad, sucking at his juice with a straw.

"But very special!" added Mom quickly. "And I think fairy school would suit you perfectly."

"But of course you may prefer vampire school," said Dad. "It's a lot more exciting."

"Is it?" asked Mom, sounding as though she did not agree at all. "How about we let Isadora decide for herself?"

Pink Rabbit jumped up and down in agreement.

"Isadora can spend one day at fairy school and one night at vampire school and decide which one she likes best," said Mom.

"But . . . ," I began.

"Fantastic idea!" exclaimed Dad.

"Well . . . okay," I said in a small voice.

I suddenly didn't want to eat breakfast anymore. I took Pink Rabbit's paw and walked slowly back up the stairs to my bedroom, thinking very hard the whole way.

"Which school would you like to go to, Pink Rabbit?" I asked. "Vampire or fairy?"

He didn't say anything because he can't talk, but he looked up at me with his beady black eyes and gave an extra little bounce.

"A rabbit school!" I replied. "I don't think those exist!"

When we got to my room, we had a tea party with my special bat-patterned tea set. Having a tea party always helps me think better. We didn't have any real tea, so we put glitter in the teacups instead, and Pink Rabbit got it all over his nose.

"You will have to learn to be more civilized once we are at school," I told him.

"I know they are very strict about manners at vampire school."

Pink Rabbit looked a little ashamed, so I patted his head and brushed the glitter off his nose.

"It doesn't matter," I said. "We can always

go to fairy school instead. I think they are more easygoing there."

Pink Rabbit seemed to like that idea.

"Also," I added, "I bet they eat more cake at fairy school. They might even have carrot cake!"

Pink Rabbit bounced up and down with excitement. Even though he can't really eat food, he likes to pretend. Carrot cake is his favorite.

I stood up and brushed the glitter off my dress.

"Oh, I just don't know!" I wailed. "I just don't know if I am more fairy or more vampire! I love magic, sunshine, and dancing around campfires, but I also love the black of night and flying among the moon and stars. It's *very* difficult. I don't know what I am or *which* school I'm going to pick!"

Pink Rabbit just shrugged and stared at me. I picked him up, and we went over to my tower window. The sky twinkled with stars. I knew Dad would be in the second-tallest tower right now, gazing at them through his expensive telescope.

"Stars are all different, you know," I said to Pink Rabbit. "Each one is unique. But they all look the same from down here."

Pink Rabbit nodded wisely, but I could see he had other things on his mind.

He was thinking about jumping out the window.

I took his pink squishy paw, and we stepped up onto the windowsill.

"Come on," I said. "Let's go for a fly among the stars before bed."

Chapter Three

FAIRY SCHOOL

Teacher: Mr. Sparkletoes

Likes: neat handwriting, butterflies, camping in the wilderness, and magic

9:00 a.m. Lesson 1—wand waving

10:30 a.m. Break time—coconut milk and organic cupcakes

11:00 a.m. Lesson 2—dancing

12:30 p.m. Lunchtime—buttercup soup with acorn pancakes

2:00 p.m. Lesson 3—flower garlands

4:00 p.m. Home time

I felt nervous the night before fairy school. I think Pink Rabbit did too. I can always tell when Pink Rabbit is nervous or excited, because he fidgets all night. He fidgeted all that night, and I almost didn't sleep a wink.

That's why I was very tired the next day when Mom came in to get me up.

"Come on, Isadora, rise and shine!" she said. "It's time for fairy school. I just know you're going to love it!"

She led me downstairs for my morning bath.

In the garden pond.

Mom loves to bathe in the pond among the lily pads, and she thinks we should all do the same.

"It's so nice to be at one with nature!"

Personally, I prefer when Dad is in charge of bath time. It is much less . . . *cold*. When Dad is in charge of bath time, he switches all the lamps off and lights lots of candles. It is very relaxing. Sometimes he makes shadow puppets dance across the walls for me too.

That's my favorite kind of bath time.

★ ★ ★

The fairy school was on top of a hill covered in flowers. It looked like a giant cupcake with windows and doors. Glitter puffed out from the giant shiny cherry on top.

"Doesn't it look wonderful?" said Mom. Then she kissed my cheek and flew away.

Fairy
School

I stood looking at the school, holding Pink Rabbit's paw. He needed me to hold his paw because everything was so new and a little scary.

My teacher was named Mr. Sparkletoes. He had pink hair that looked like the icing on a cupcake.

"Good morning, class," he said. "Today we are going to learn how to use a magic wand!"

I had always wanted a wand of my very own. Suddenly, I knew fairy school was for me! After all, who doesn't want a glittery wand that can grant wishes?

"We are going to make wonderful things appear," said Mr. Sparkletoes. "All you need to do is wave your wand and *imagine*. You should all be naturals at it!"

He handed everyone a sparkly silver wand.

At once, every fairy began to wave

their wand in the air. Nice things began to appear around the classroom. Little kittens, giant bowls of ice cream, striped lollipops, towering birthday cakes, freshly squeezed lemonade . . .

"What shall we wish for, Pink Rabbit?" I
asked.

Pink Rabbit bounced up and down beside
me.

"Carrot cake!" I said. "Good idea."

I imagined a huge, towering cake covered in creamy icing and decorated with little candied carrots.

WHOOSH! I waved my wand.

A single carrot dropped out of the air and rolled across the floor.

I frowned. "That was not what I was imagining," I said.

I closed my eyes and thought of the cake again. I could see it very clearly.

I knew *exactly* what it was supposed to look like. It had five layers and a little candy rabbit on top.

32

I waved my wand again.

WHOOSH!

Still, no cake appeared. Instead, the carrot started to grow. It rolled around on the floor, getting bigger and bigger all the time.

"Oh dear," I said to Pink Rabbit. I looked around for Mr. Sparkletoes, but he was busy taste-testing a fairy's cake over on the other side of the room.

The carrot was now HUGE!

"Stop growing!" I said to it. "Stop!"

But the carrot did not stop. It kept getting bigger and bigger and bigger.

"Mr. Sparkletoes!" I called. But he didn't hear me over the excited chatter of all the fairies.

I stared at the giant carrot. A few of the fairies nearby had noticed it now. They were pointing and laughing.

It was embarrassing.

I waved my wand at the carrot once

more. There was a **WHOOSH** and a shower of sparks.

Stop growing! I thought. *Turn into a cake.*

The carrot stopped growing.

But it did not turn into a cake. Instead, it sprouted a pair of black bat's wings and began to flap itself into the air.

I shouted:

"MR. SPARKLETOES!!!"

Finally, he turned around. Just in time to see the giant carrot zooming around the classroom, crashing from wall to wall and destroying everything in its way. Cake and lemonade exploded everywhere, splattering the walls and splashing all over the floor.

"TAKE COVER!" shouted Mr. Sparkletoes, immediately leaping underneath his desk at the front of the classroom.

All the other fairies followed his lead, diving under their desks too.

I crouched down under mine and listened to the bangs and crashes going on above my head.

This is all my fault! I thought, reaching out for Pink Rabbit's paw.

But Pink Rabbit's paw was not there. And neither was Pink Rabbit.

Where was he?!

I peered out from under the desk through the lemonade rain and shower of cake crumbs. My heart felt tight in my chest. What if he had been squashed?

But then I saw him! He was on the other side of the room, opening one of the big classroom windows.

What a clever rabbit! I thought.

The window swung open, and a cool summery breeze floated into the room. The carrot stopped in midair. It did a somersault. Then it pointed its nose toward the open window and rocketed out into the sky, scattering a trail of cake crumbs and lollipops behind it.

Everything went quiet for a second, and no one said anything.

Then Mr. Sparkletoes got out from under his desk and smoothed down his shirt.

"Come on, everyone," he said. "Get out from under your desks. Honestly! Hiding under your desks because of a carrot!"

Then he said, "Isadora, I don't think you have the best fairy skill for wand waving."

Oh well, I thought. *Maybe I am completely a vampire after all.*

Chapter Four

The next lesson was ballet.

I have taken ballet lessons since I was three, so I wasn't worried about messing up this class.

We all went to change into our tutus.

I *love* my ballet tutu. It is my second-favorite thing, after Pink Rabbit. It is as black as midnight, with silver stars and black glitter.

It makes me feel **MYSTICAL** and **MAGICAL**.

Sometimes I wear it just for fun when I'm at home.

I put it on, and then I noticed that all the other fairies were staring at me. And so was Mr. Sparkletoes.

"You can't wear that," they all said. "It's black!"

"But I like black," I said. "Black is the color of the sky at night. Black is a mystical and magical color. And look how it sparkles!"

"But it's black," said Mr. Sparkletoes. "We fairies wear pink ballet outfits. It's the rule."

I was made to change out of my tutu and into a puffy pink one. It just wasn't the same.

I messed up in the pink tutu. I missed my steps, and I was the worst in the class. I just didn't feel like my mystical, magical self.

"Oh dear," I said to Pink Rabbit. "I think maybe I am more vampire than I thought."

For lunch we had buttercup soup and acorn pancakes.

"*Yum,*" said all the fairies. "We *love* acorn pancakes and buttercup soup. They taste like trees and flowers!"

I wasn't sure I wanted my food to taste like trees and flowers, but I was very hungry, so I ate it all up. It wasn't too bad.

But nowhere near as good as peanut butter on toast.

The last lesson of the day was flower-garland making.

"It's almost midsummer," said Mr. Sparkletoes. "A very important event on the fairy calendar. We will go into the magic woodland behind the school and look for branches and flowers to make crowns! Then we will wear them next week to dance around a bonfire."

"Ooh!" said all the fairies.

"Yes," said Mr. Sparkletoes. "It is a wonderful way to be close to nature. Off we go. Barefoot, everyone!"

Everyone took off their shoes, and then we all followed Mr. Sparkletoes out of the school to the magic woodland.

"Here we are," he said. "Now let's go searching!"

I really wanted to do a good job after the disastrous magic-wand and ballet lessons.

I'll show them, I thought. *I'll make the best crown they've ever seen!* I began to collect the biggest and most beautiful flowers I could find. Then I wove in some leaves and twigs. Pink Rabbit looked on in approval.

"Five minutes left!" said Mr. Sparkletoes. "Then I will come and look at what you've done."

I really wanted my crown to be the best. What else could I add?

I spotted some brightly colored toad-stools growing in a ring nearby.

"These will look like jewels!" I said to

Pink Rabbit. I quickly picked some and wove them into the crown.

"Beautiful! Look, Pink Rabbit, I am the queen!"

But when Mr. Sparkletoes saw what I had done, he was not happy at all.

"Isadora Moon!" he said. "You have just ruined a sacred fairy ring!"

I blinked.

"Has no one ever told you," said Mr. Sparkletoes, "never, *ever* to pick toadstools from a fairy ring? Besides, those are poisonous."

I looked down at my hands and saw that they were covered in itchy red spots.

"Take that crown off at once!" ordered Mr. Sparkletoes.

 "You'd better go and get some magic cream from the school nurse," he added.

I quickly ripped the crown off my head and threw it onto the ground. I felt my eyes fill with tears.

"I didn't know," I said. "I didn't know because I am not a fairy—I am a vampire!"

Then I turned around and ran back toward the school and refused to say another word until Mom came to pick me up at the end of the day.

Chapter Five

"How was your day?" asked Mom when she saw me. "Did you have a nice time? Isn't fairy school wonderful?"

And I said that, no, it was not wonderful at all, and that actually I didn't think I was a fairy. I was just a vampire.

Mom looked disappointed.

"You're probably just tired," she said. "I'm sure you'll feel different tomorrow."

We went home and had breakfast with Dad.

He was very happy to hear that I was a vampire.

"I did think so all along," he said as he slurped down his red juice.

After breakfast, it was bedtime. I was so tired from my day at fairy school that I didn't even remember to brush my teeth. I just snuggled with Pink Rabbit under our starry quilt and fell asleep.

When I woke up, it was morning and the sun was streaming through my tower window.

"Come on, Pink Rabbit!" I said, pushing him out of bed. "It's vampire school tonight!"

I got dressed, and then we slid down the banister to the kitchen.

Dad was just coming in from his nighttime flying. He was yawning and looking tired.

Mom was busy picking apples off the tree in the kitchen. She was turning them into glasses of apple juice with her wand.

I sat down at the table and started to butter my toast.

"Are you looking forward to vampire school tonight?" asked Dad hopefully.

"Oh yes!" I said. "I think I'm going to like vampire school."

Dad looked pleased. He yawned and glanced at the clock on the wall.

"Well, you'd better go back to bed after breakfast," he said. "You must sleep all through the day so that you're nice and fresh for the evening. Just like I do!"

I stared at him.

"But I just got out of bed!" I said in astonishment. "I'm not tired!"

"You will be tired at school if you don't sleep today," said Dad. "Come on, finish your toast and go up to bed."

So I finished my toast, but verrrry slowly. And then I walked up the stairs to my room.

Verrrry slowly. And then I got back into my
pajamas verrrry slowly, and then I sat in my
bed and stared at the sun coming through the
window.

How on earth was I supposed to fall asleep now?

It was a very bright day, and the birds were singing loudly outside. The human children on their way to school were being noisy too. After a few minutes, I got up and tried to block out the light with my quilt. It didn't really work.

"MOOOM!" I shouted down the stairs.

Mom came hurrying up.

"What's the matter?" she said.

"It's too bright," I complained.

Mom waved her wand, and a pair of dark curtains appeared across my window.

"It's too loud," I said. "I can hear the birds."

Mom made me a pair of earplugs.

"I'm thirsty," I said.

Mom poured me a glass of apple juice.

"I think I need the bathroom."

"Well, you'd better go, then," sighed Mom.

By the time it was evening, I had not slept a wink. But I had drunk thirteen glasses of apple juice and been to the bathroom too many times to count.

I suddenly felt very tired. I could hardly keep my eyes open. Nor could Pink Rabbit.

"We're very sleepy," I told Dad. "Maybe we should just go to bed."

"Nonsense," said Dad. "You've been asleep all day! Once you see how exciting vampire school is, you won't want to go to bed!"

Chapter Six

VAMPIRE SCHOOL

Teacher: Countess Darkfang

Likes: twirly handwriting, black bats, and slicked-back, shiny hair

10:00 p.m. Lesson 1—flying in formation

11:30 p.m. Break time—red juice

1:00 a.m. Lesson 2—bat training

3:00 a.m. Lunchtime—tomato soup with tomato sandwiches and beetroot crisps

4:30 a.m. Lesson 3—grooming

7:00 a.m. Home time

Vampire school was also on a hill, but it was not covered with flowers and it was not built in the shape of a pink cupcake.

It was a tall black castle with bats flying around its spires and towers. Thunder and lightning cracked through the sky behind it.

Pink Rabbit shivered, so I held his paw tight. I could tell he was frightened. He doesn't like thunderstorms.

"Isn't it wonderful?" said Dad. Then he opened his black cloak and flew away into the sky, whooping with delight.

My teacher was named Countess Darkfang. She was very tall and had spiky red nails.

"Good evening, class," she said. "Tonight we are going to learn how to fly like real vampires. We are going to SWOOSH and GLIDE and WHIZ across the moon! We are going to make some neat formation shapes in the sky. We will start with an arrow shape. A nice spiky arrow."

Oh goody, I thought. I knew how to fly already, and also I had something the other vampire children did not: wings! This would be easy.

"Follow me!" said Countess Darkfang. She lifted out her cloak and shot into the air with lightning speed.

One by one, the other vampires followed. SWOOSH, GLIDE, WHIZ.

Then it was my turn. But as I rose into
the air, I realized that I wasn't swooshing or
gliding or whizzing. I was . . . flapping.

Flap, flap, flap went my wings. And they didn't go nearly as fast as the others'. They acted more like . . . fairy wings. How had I not noticed before?

"Come on, Isadora!" shouted Countess Darkfang. "You're getting left behind!"

I flapped my wings harder, trying to keep up. I could see all the other little vampires far ahead of me, circling around the big, bright moon.

"**ARROW!**" screeched Countess Darkfang.

All the other vampires arranged themselves into the shape of an arrow, leaving a space on the end for me.

"Come on, Isadora!" they called.

I flapped as hard as I could and eventually reached the space at the end of the arrow shape. I was just getting my breath back when Countess Darkfang said:

"NOW ZOOM!"

Suddenly, the arrow formation shot forward, and I was left alone again in the middle of the sky.

This was *exhausting*.

"Wait!" I cried, flapping my wings as hard as I could. "Wait for me!"

"STOP, EVERYONE!" shrieked Countess Darkfang suddenly. "We must wait for Isadora."

The others immediately came to a stop in the sky, still in their perfect arrow formation. Not a hair was out of place on their shiny heads.

I continued to flap along, but I wasn't used to flying this fast. Now I couldn't stop! I crashed right into the vampire at the back of the arrow, my wings tangling in his cape so that we rolled into a ball and began to plummet toward the ground.

"Help!" I cried as
we spun around
and around,
stars rushing
past our eyes.

"EMERGENCY!"

screeched Countess

Darkfang. She gathered her cape and shot

down toward us. Luckily, vampires are very

fast fliers. She grabbed on to my dress just

before we hit the ground.

"That was close!" she said as she set us

both upright. "I think that's enough flying

for now."

Pink Rabbit wiped his paw across his

forehead in relief.

"I am not sure flying is your greatest talent, Isadora," said Countess Darkfang.

I hung my head. Maybe I *was* more fairy than vampire.

Chapter Seven

After the flying lesson, it was time for a snack. Countess Darkfang gave out cartons of red juice to everyone.

"Yum!" said all the little vampires.

"Yuck!" I said. "It's *tomato* juice!"

74

"Of course it is," said Countess Darkfang. "That's what we vampires like to drink. Delicious!"

I looked at Pink Rabbit, and Pink Rabbit looked at me.

"I think," I whispered, "that maybe I'm not a vampire after all. . . ."

Then I yawned. A big yawn. I was so tired.

"Now!" said Countess Darkfang. "It is time for the bat-training lesson. Follow me!"

She led us all along a dark, windy hallway to a big room where there were hundreds, maybe *thousands*, of bats in cages.

"Bats make wonderful vampire pets," said

Countess Darkfang. "They are especially useful for delivering mail."

She gestured around her at the bats flapping in their cages.

"You may all choose one to be your own special pet," she said.

I looked around the room. I suddenly felt excited. I *love* bats. We have twenty-seven of them in our attic. I liked the idea of having my own special one as a pet.

I peered into the
cages. There were big
bats and small bats, scrawny bats and sleek
bats. Which one should I choose?

In the end, I decided on a medium one
with silky fur and beady black eyes.

"I will call him Buttons," I said to Pink
Rabbit. "Don't you think that's nice?"

But for some reason, Pink Rabbit did not
look very happy.

"Now!" said Countess Darkfang. "The
first rule of bat training is to never let your
bat out of its cage outside or when the window is open. Otherwise it might fly away."

Everyone looked around the room to
check that the windows were closed.

"Of course," continued the countess, "once your bat is fully trained like mine, it will never fly away." She smiled smugly and stroked her own pet bat, which was very large and had fur as black as midnight.

"You may let your bat out now," she said.

I opened the door of the little cage, and Buttons flew into the air.

"Good," said Countess Darkfang. "Let's begin! The first thing we are going to teach our bats is how to do a somersault in the air." She pointed at her own bat and swizzled her finger at it. Immediately, the bat turned a perfect somersault.

"Now you try it," she said to the class.

I pointed my finger at Buttons and made

a circular motion. Buttons turned upside down in the air.

"Almost!" I said excitedly. "Pink Rabbit, did you see that?"

But Pink Rabbit didn't hear me. He was busy turning perfect somersaults on the floor.

"The second thing we are going to do," said Countess Darkfang, "is teach our pet to sit neatly on our shoulder." She snapped her fingers, and her bat immediately flew down onto her left shoulder.

I snapped my finger at Buttons.

But before he could do anything, Pink

Rabbit came leaping through the air and landed on my shoulder with a thump.

"Hey!" I said. "Pink Rabbit, you have to get down!"

But Pink Rabbit did not want to get down. He held on to my neck with his pink paws and dug his soft feet firmly into my collarbone.

"You really do," I said, "or we'll get into trouble." I picked him off me and set him on the floor.

I turned my attention back to Buttons and snapped my fingers at him again.

"Come on," I urged him.

But Buttons didn't seem very interested in coming to sit on my shoulder. He was suddenly fascinated with something over on the other side of the room. What was it? I turned to see and then gasped.

The castle window! It was swinging wide open!

Oh NO! I thought as the air suddenly became full of the sound of flapping wings.

All the pet bats, including Buttons, started to dash toward the open window.

WHOOSH! they went. FLAP! SWISH! FREEDOM!

"ARGHHH!" screeched Countess Darkfang. **"WHO HAS OPENED THE WINDOW?"** She lifted her cape and leapt across the room to close it.

But it was too late.

The bats were gone.

I glanced across at Pink Rabbit. He was standing by the open window looking very pleased with himself.

"Isadora Moon!" Countess Darkfang shouted. "That Pink Rabbit of yours is a **LIABILITY. A NUISANCE!** I am hereby **BANNING** him from vampire school!"

"But . . . ," I said.

"No buts," said Countess Darkfang. "After today he is never, **EVER** allowed back."

Then she picked up her cape and swished out of the room to the lunch hall.

I thought Pink Rabbit didn't look sorry at all.

Chapter Eight

After lunch, which was more red food (tomato sandwiches and tomato soup with beet chips—yuck!), it was time for the last lesson of the day. Grooming.

"Grooming is **VERY** important," said Countess Darkfang as she walked around the classroom handing out little silver hand

mirrors, spiky hairbrushes, and pots of gloopy hair gel. "Vampires must look their best. Shiny, neat hair is extremely important. It's the rule." She patted her own perfect hair proudly. There was so much gel in it that it made a TAP TAP sound when she touched it.

All the other vampires began to comb their already neat and shiny hair, smiling as they did so.

I picked up the hairbrush. This was not going to be easy. My hair is quite . . . wild.

I put the hairbrush to my head.

A minute later, it was stuck!

"Countess Darkfang," I called. "The hairbrush is stuck in my hair!"

Countess Darkfang came hurrying over, tutting loudly. She gave the hairbrush a little pull, but it didn't budge.

"Your hair is just too tangled," she complained. She yanked a little harder.

"Ouch!" I said.

And then a bit harder . . .

"OUCH!" I yelled.

At last the hairbrush came out. And so did a big clump of my hair.

"Let's try the gel instead," said Countess Darkfang. She scooped a large handful from the pot and began to smooth it over my head.

"This'll do it," she said.

But the gel did not do it. My hair would just not stay down. I peered into the hand mirror and watched as Countess Darkfang tried to flatten it. Every time she tried to smooth a piece of hair into place, it would ping right back up again.

Ping, ping, PING!

"Hmm." Countess Darkfang frowned. "Isadora, your hair is **WILD!**"

I smiled sleepily. I don't mind my hair being wild. In fact, I quite like it. I closed my eyes as Countess Darkfang continued to cover my head with handfuls of the

gloopy gel. It felt quite soothing. And I was so sleepy. . . .

"I *will* tame it," I heard her say as I drifted off. "I *will*! This is not satisfactory. . . ."

And then, before I knew it, I was fast asleep.

Chapter Nine

Dad was not very impressed when he came to pick me up at the end of the night.

"You're not supposed to fall asleep at vampire school, Isadora!" he said.

"I know," I said sadly. "I think maybe I'm not a vampire at all."

Dad looked disappointed.

"I expect you'll feel differently after you've slept a bit," he said hopefully. "Let's go home."

So we flew home together, and I went straight to bed like Dad does every morning.

I slept through the whole morning and didn't wake up until three o'clock!

It felt very strange.

When I got up, Mom was waiting for me in the kitchen. She had made me a sandwich. I could tell she had used magic to make it, because every time I bit into it the flavor changed. First it was ham, then peanut butter, then cucumber, then . . .

"**YUCK!** Tomatoes!" I yelled.

Mom's shortcuts don't always pay off.

94

"Oh dear," she said. "Sorry. I still haven't got that spell quite right. Let me try again."

"It's okay," I said. "I'm not hungry anymore."

"So how was vampire school?" Mom asked. "Did you like it better than fairy school?"

"I'm not sure . . . ," I said. "I still don't know if I am more fairy or vampire."

"Oh," said Mom. "I see."

I took a handful of cereal and wandered into the garden with Pink Rabbit. Through the fence, we could see the human children walking home along the pavement. Some of them were scruffy, and some of them were neat. Some of them were loud, and some of them were quiet. Some of them were tall, and some of them were short. Some of them were big, and some of them were small. And some of them were just in between.

And the thing was, none of them seemed to mind!

I suddenly remembered what Dad had told me about the stars in the sky. How every one of them is different, but how they are all just as beautiful, and I thought, *Maybe it doesn't matter if I am a little different. Different can be beautiful too.*

I pressed my face closer to the fence, and one of the children saw me. He had blond hair and lots of freckles and a big smile.

He said, "Hey, you, what's your name?"

I didn't say anything because I suddenly felt very shy.

But the boy didn't leave. He came over to where I was and gazed up at my house.

"Cool house!" he said.

Then he spotted my wings. "Cool wings!" he said. "Can you really fly with them?"

I nodded and fluttered a few inches off the ground.

"Awesome!" shouted the boy.

The other children were coming over now.

"WOW!" they said. "We've always wanted to talk to you!"

"Really?" I said in astonishment.

99

"Oh yes," said the boy. "We walk past your house every day on our way to school. We've seen you up in that tower window."

"*And* we've seen a fairy here!" said a little girl with pigtails who was busy munching on a peanut butter sandwich. "A fairy with

pink hair! Me and my friends are always trying to peek in to see her."

"Oh, that's just my mom," I said.

"Some of us have seen a vampire." The boy shuddered. "A really scary vampire with a black cape and pointy teeth. Some kids in our class are too scared to walk past your house, you know." He puffed out his chest. "Not me!"

I laughed.

"That's just my dad," I said. "He's not scary at all!"

"So there really are fairies and vampires living here?" the children asked. "Really?"

"Yes!" I said. "Really! And there is also a vampire-fairy living here . . . ME!"

"A vampire-fairy!" said the children.
"That's even better!"

"I wish *I* was a vampire-fairy," said a girl
with pink plastic clips in her curly hair.

Suddenly, I felt very proud to be me.

"My name is Isadora," I told the children.

"That's a nice name," said the curly-haired

girl. "My name is Zoe, and that's Sashi." She pointed to the girl with pigtails.

"And I'm Bruno," said the boy. "So what school do you go to? Is it a special school for vampire-fairies?"

"Well," I began, "I . . ."

But just then I heard a sound from the house.

"ISADOOOORA!"

It was Mom calling me inside.

"I have to go," I said to the children. "But it was really nice to meet you! Maybe we can talk through the fence again one day? I can bring us peanut butter sandwiches!"

"Oh yes!" said all the children. "Please come back! We can have a picnic. And bring

your Pink Rabbit again too—he's so funny!"

"Peanut butter sandwiches are my favorite," said Sashi.

"Mine too!" I said. "I like them with apple juice."

"That sounds tasty!" said Bruno.

"**ISADOOOORA!** What are you doing?" called Mom again.

"I really have to go!" I said.

I said goodbye to the children and ran back to the house with Pink Rabbit bouncing joyfully along behind me.

My run turned into a skip and then a skippity-hop. I couldn't help it. I suddenly felt so happy.

Chapter
Ten

"There you are," said Mom when I got inside.

"Oh good." Dad yawned. It was still too early for him to be awake, so he was wearing his sunglasses.

"We have decided to see if you can go

to *both* schools," Mom said. "It's the perfect solution!"

"But . . . ," I said.

"You can go to fairy school in the morning, come home for a quick nap, and then go to vampire school at night," she said.

"But . . . ," I said, "I don't *want* to do that."

Mom looked surprised. "Why not?" she said.

"I've thought of a much better solution. . . . I want to go to **REGULAR HUMAN SCHOOL!**"

Mom and Dad both gasped.

"Oh no no NO!" they exclaimed. "Why on earth would you want to go there? You are magical! You are special! You need to go to a special school. It's vampire school or fairy school."

I shook my head. "No," I said. "I want to go to regular school."

"But it's full of humans!" said Dad, astonished. "Humans are *so* weird. They

hardly get any fresh air. They sit around watching boxes all day. They eat beige food, and they use screens to talk to each other. . . ."

"They can't even fly!" added Mom.

"Well, I just spoke to some of the children, and they were very nice. There was one named Bruno and one named Zoe and one named—"

"You *spoke* to them!" gasped Dad in horror.

"But . . . but . . . they're not like you," said Mom. "You are different."

"I know," I said. "But they were all different too. Like the stars that Dad looks at through his telescope. And they didn't mind that I am not a full vampire or a full fairy. In fact, they thought it was *interesting*."

"Hmm . . . ," said Dad. "Humans are very odd."

"Well, I like them," I said. "I'm starting

to think that it's *you* two who are a little strange!"

"Well!" said Mom, tapping the apple tree with her wand so that it started to grow oranges instead.

"Really!" said Dad, pushing his sunglasses up.

"Yes," I told them. "But you know, I think that's good. Things would be very boring otherwise."

Pink Rabbit nodded wisely beside me.

"And so," I continued firmly, "I have decided that regular school is the perfect place for me!"

"Hmm," said Mom, picking an orange off the tree.

"Are you *sure* you wouldn't rather go to vampire school?" Dad asked.

"I am sure," I told him.

"And are you *sure* you wouldn't rather go to fairy school?" added Mom.

"Yes!" I said.

"Well then," said Dad, "maybe regular school *is* the place for you."

"Maybe it *could* be the perfect place for you," said Mom, holding her arms out to me for a hug.

I smiled, and Pink Rabbit bounced up and down beside me.

"I know it is!" I told them happily. "Human school is the perfect place for a vampire-fairy like me!"

Harriet Muncaster

Harriet Muncaster, that's me! I'm the author and illustrator of Isadora Moon.

Yes, really! I love anything teeny-tiny, anything starry, and everything glittery.

Sink your fangs into
Isadora Moon's next adventure!

It all started one sunny morning. I came downstairs to find Mom waving her wand around in the kitchen. She had made a flower-patterned tent appear, and it was sitting in the middle of the floor.

Mom smiled at me as I came into the room. "There you are!" she said. "What do you think of this?" She pointed at the tent. "Do you like the pattern? It's for you. We're going camping!"

"What?!" said Dad.

"Camping!" Mom repeated. "We're going camping at the beach. I booked it this morning."

"I," said Dad primly, "do not *do* camping."

"Oh, don't be silly!" said Mom. "You'll love it! There's nothing better than waking up outdoors with the morning sunshine blasting into your tent . . . cooking on a campfire . . . playing in the sand. It's wonderful to be so close to nature!"

Dad did not look convinced.

I walked around the tent in the middle of the floor, inspecting it and lifting the flap to look inside.

"So what do you think?" Mom asked again.

"I'm not sure about the color," I admitted. "It's a bit *too* pink and flowery. . . ."

"Okay," said Mom. "How about this?" She waved her wand again, and the tent changed to a black-and-white-striped pattern.